For Sabina, who so bravely supplies this cactus with hugs

SIMON & SCHUSTER
BOOKS FOR YOUNG READERS is a
trademark of Simon & Schuster, Inc. ~
For information about special discounts for bulk purchases, please
contact Simon & Schuster Special Sales at 1-866-506-1949 or
business@simonandschuster.com. ~ The Simon & Schuster Speakers
Bureau can bring authors to your live event. For more information or to book an event,
contact the Simon & Schuster Speakers Bureau at 1-866-248-3049 or visit our website at
www.simonspeakers.com.

SIMON & SCHUSTER
BOOKS FOR YOUNG
READERS ~ An imprint of Simon & Schuster
Children's Publishing Division ~ 1230 Avenue of the Americas,
New York, New York 10020 ~ Copyright © 2019 by Carter
Goodrich ~ All rights reserved, including the right of
reproduction in whole or in part in any form.

Book design
by Dan Potash ~
The text for this book
was set in Mildew. ~ The illustrations
for this book were rendered in watercolor.
~ Manufactured in China ~ 0119 SCP ~
First Edition ~ 10 9 8 7 6 5 4 3 2 1

Library
of Congress
Cataloging-in-Publication
Data ~ Names: Goodrich, Carter,
author, illustrator ~ Title: Nobody hugs a cactus / Carter
Goodrich. ~ Description: First edition. New York : Simon
& Schuster Books for Young Readers, [2018] ~ Summary:
Hank, a cactus who is as prickly on the inside as he is on the
outside, decides he wants a hug. ~ Identifiers: LCCN 2017017314
(print) LCCN 2017035294 (eBook) ~ ISBN 9781534400900 (hardcover)
ISBN 9781534400917 (eBook) ~ Subjects: CYAC: Cactus–Fiction. Mood
(Psychology)–Fiction. Tumbleweeds–Fiction. Animals–Fiction. Hugging–
Fiction. ~ Classification: LCC PZ7.G61447 (eBook) LCC PZ7.G61447 Nob 2018
(print) DDC [E]–dc23 ~ LC record available at https://lccn.loc.gov/2017017314

Nobody Hugs a Cactus

Carter Goodrich

Simon & Schuster Books for Young Readers
New York London Toronto Sydney New Delhi

Hank lived in a pot.

The pot sat in a window.

The window looked out at the empty desert.

It was hot, dry, peaceful, and quiet.

Just the way Hank liked it.

But every now and then, somebody would
interrupt Hank's peace and quiet.

"Hi, Hank!" Rosie the Tumbleweed called out.
"Isn't it a beautiful day?"

Hank ignored her. He just wanted to be left alone.

"Okay, so long!" said Rosie cheerfully, and she tumbled away.

Hank was happy again.

But just as he was beginning to relax . . .

"Hello!" shouted a tortoise.

"Private property!" yelled Hank. "Keep out!"
The tortoise was so frightened, he hid in his shell.

Hank was still yelling at the tortoise when a jackrabbit dashed by.

"Hiya, Prickles!" she shouted.

"My name isn't Prickles!" Hank yelled back. "And stay out of my yard!"

"Tumbleweeds, tortoises, jackrabbits . . . What's next?" said Hank.

A coyote came loping by.

"No dogs allowed!" Hank yelled.

"I'm not a dog," said the coyote. "And YOU are as prickly on the inside as you are on the outside."

Before Hank could yell back at the coyote, a cowboy strode past.
"Keep off the grass!" shouted Hank.

"What grass?" said the cowboy.
"Seems to me, somebody needs a hug.
Too bad nobody hugs a cactus."

"Hi!" said a lizard.

"Who invited you?" said Hank. "And just in case you're wondering, I don't want a hug."

"That's good," said the lizard, "because I don't want to give you one."

Then he skittered away.

An owl landed on the roof.

"If you're looking for a hug," said Hank,
"well ... I *guess* I could give you one."

"Whooo . . . me?" said the owl. "You must be joking!"
And for the first time, Hank began to feel a little lonely.

The next morning Hank was feeling more sad on the inside than prickly.

Maybe a hug wouldn't be so bad after all.

The wind began to pick up.

An old cup blew by and stuck to Hank's face.

His arms were too short to get it off.

"Great," said Hank.

After a while, Rosie came bouncing by.

"I'll get it off you, Hank!" she shouted, and she jumped
up to knock the cup off Hank's face.
Then she tumbled away.

Hank didn't have time to thank Rosie.
He felt bad about all the other times he
had been so rude to her.

So he came up with a plan.

Hank decided to grow the best flower he could,
and then give it to Rosie as a thank-you gift.

It took days, but at last it was ready.
He couldn't wait for Rosie to pass by again.

When at last she finally did come bouncing back, Hank held out the flower.

"Look, Rosie!" he said. "I grew it just for you!"

Rosie was so surprised, she jumped up
and gave Hank a great big hug!

It felt so nice, Hank didn't want to let go.
And as things turned out, he couldn't.
Rosie and Hank had become stuck together.

But they didn't care.

After all, it's better to be stuck in a hug than stuck all alone.